The Third-Story Cat

 Little, Brown and Company
Boston/Toronto

Leslie Baker

The Third-Story Cat

For Emma

First Edition

Library of Congress Cataloging-in-Publication Data
Baker, Leslie A.
  The third-story cat.

  Summary: A house cat with a longing to visit the park across the
street "escapes" her comfortable apartment, meets a streetwise cat, and
is given a tour that results in a hair-raising encounter that sends her
rushing home to stay—at least until tomorrow.
  [1. Cats—Fiction] I. Title.
PZ7.B1744Th 1987   [E]   86-20142
ISBN 0-316-07832-8
10 9 8 7 6 5 4 3
                Designed by Trisha Hanlon

Published simultaneously in Canada
by Little, Brown & Company (Canada) Limited

Printed in the United States of America

Alice was a third-story cat. She lived in a small apartment in the city with a girl named Annie. Every day Alice would look out the window and wish that she could visit the park across the street—even just once.

One spring day Alice got her chance. Annie had left the kitchen window open just a bit. Alice squeezed through without anyone seeing her. She was free!

Carefully, she crept along the narrow ledge. It was hard to keep her balance in the strong wind.

Alice stopped short. Her path was blocked by a window box full
of geraniums.

She tiptoed through them and almost lost her balance when a butterfly rose from the flowers and startled her.

Alice kept going until the ledge came to an end. The street below
looked very far away. What would she do?

Alice bravely leaped onto the roof of the building next door.

As she landed she frightened a small bird taking a puddle bath.
Alice was tempted to stay and investigate the bird, but then she
heard something rustling in a nearby tree.

It was a tiger cat, sitting on a branch. He winked at Alice and disappeared into the leaves. Curious, Alice followed him down the tree.

On the ground, the two cats got acquainted.

Then off they went—across the street and through the park gates.

Alice had reached the park at last!

Happily she rolled in the flower beds.

Alice had a wonderful time. She followed the tiger cat to the
fountain, where they stopped to fish.

They prowled around some people finishing lunch and found the perfect picnic under a bench.

The two cats paraded past the grandmothers, hoping to get stroked.

They joined some children playing marbles.

After their jaunt, Alice decided to take a sunbath. Her friend wasn't tired, and he played tag with some squirrels.

While resting, Alice heard an angry noise. A big dog had come out
of the bushes and was growling at the tiger cat.

Alice was frightened and ran the other way. But the dog spotted
Alice and chased after her, nipping at her tail.

Over and under, round and round they went, until Alice escaped
by jumping onto a statue. The dog ran in circles, barking at her.

By the time the dog finally gave up, it was getting dark. Alice
jumped down and began to head home. On her way out of the
park she looked for the tiger cat, but he was nowhere in sight.

Alice crossed the street and climbed back up the tree. There, at the top, was her friend. He winked at her, and she twitched her tail in response as she hurried on.

Alice leaped back onto the rooftop, then to the ledge, and stepped through the geraniums.

At last she could see her window. But it was closed! She
meowed loudly.

Annie's worried face appeared at the window. She had been searching everywhere for Alice. "Where have you been?" Annie asked as Alice hopped inside.

Alice just purred. She was glad to be a third-story cat again.

At least for now.